Puffin Books
.Editor: Kaye Webb

The New Adventures of Galldora

Marybell was very fond of her rag doll Galldora, in spite of her stuffing being weak and her mouth crookedly sewn on, because Galldora had been made by her favourite uncle on one of his sea voyages.

It seems as if Galldora had voyaging in her blood, for in this second book of her adventures she goes to all sorts of new places and gets into worse scrapes than ever before. She is left out in the woods for three days, and is stuck up in a tree in a rooks' nest, and even becomes quite a heroine when she saves Marybell and her father from drowning at sea. She also hides an important document from thieves, after her first trip in an aeroplane. But the very oddest thing that happens to her is to be baked in a rabbit pie!

'I really don't see any child (between four and seven) resisting Galldora. The author is one of the rare people who can write simply without being either monotonous or silly.' – Margery Fisher

The New Adventures of Galldora

Modwena Sedgwick

Illustrations by Diana John

Puffin Books

Puffin Books, Penguin Books Ltd,
Harmondsworth, Middlesex, England
Penguin Books, 625 Madison Avenue,
New York, New York 10022, U.S.A.
Penguin Books Canada Ltd, 2801 John Street,
Markham, Ontario, Canada
Penguin Books Australia Ltd, Ringwood,
Victoria, Australia

First published by Harrap 1961
Published in Puffin Books 1970
Reprinted 1971, 1974, 1977
Copyright © Modwena Sedgwick, 1961

Made and printed in Great Britain by
Hazell Watson & Viney Ltd, Aylesbury, Bucks
Set in Monotype Baskerville

Except in the United States of America, this
book is sold subject to the condition that
it shall not, by way of trade or otherwise, be lent,
re-sold, hired out, or otherwise circulated without
the publisher's prior consent in any form of
binding or cover other than that in which it is
published and without a similar condition
including this condition being imposed on the
subsequent purchaser

Contents

The Heroine 7

Galldora and the Woods-beyond 19

Galldora and the Rabbit Pie 29

Galldora and the Mermaid 49

Galldora and the Rooks 68

Galldora and the Important Document 74

Galldora and the Train Ride 92

The Heroine

One day there was a great squeaking and chattering among the toys in the nursery. It was not surprising, because Marybell had told them that next day her daddy was taking her to the sea, and they could all come too.

Now, one doll, Galldora, the rag doll, said nothing. She sat dreaming on the window-sill, dreaming of sea and sands. She did not expect that she would be taken. For, as Marybell had so often told her, 'You are a disgrace to look at, Galldora.'

Poor Galldora, her stuffing was weak, and her mouth was sewn on crookedly. But – well, Marybell never had the heart to throw her away, because she had been made by her favourite uncle, Uncle Jack.

Uncle Jack sailed on ships all over the world, and the ships took cargoes of bananas from here to there, and pineapples and dates, and china and glass, and other things as well. Uncle Jack was known as 'Sparks' on his ship, and he was very important and knew all about sending out messages over the air. When Uncle Jack wasn't sending out messages or receiving messages, and when there wasn't a gale on, or a typhoon, or other sea troubles, Uncle Jack found time to make rugs and even to knit. But though Uncle Jack made ever so many rugs and knitted a great many socks, he only made one doll, and that was Galldora.

So Galldora was very special. Still, as she looked so queer, she was usually left sitting on the nursery window-sill when Marybell took the dolls and teddies on a special treat.

Next morning Marybell came into the nursery and collected up all her dolls and teddies, and the stuffed cat, Bobo, her spade, bucket, and the small shrimping-net. She put them in a pile in the middle of the floor, but she left Galldora where she was.

'Oh, but, Marybell, dear,' said Marybell's mother, 'you can't take all those. I said just one or two.'

Marybell looked very sad. 'But they all

want to come,' she said. Marybell was very understanding.

'Just take one doll and one teddy,' said Marybell's mother firmly.

'But what about Bobo?' said Marybell.

'But cats don't like the sea, Marybell,' said Marybell's mother.

'He would like the drive in the car,' said Marybell, 'and the teddies like being buried in the sand, and the French doll hasn't seen an English seaside, and Lulu likes sun-bathing, and so does Queenie, and Pansy wants to show off her new dress, and –'

'Really, dear,' said Marybell's mother, 'seven bears and ten dolls and a stuffed cat, are rather a lot.'

'Couldn't they just sit in the car? I won't take them all out, really I won't,' begged Marybell.

'Oh, very well,' said Marybell's mother. Then she said: 'But no more, mind you.'

Marybell suddenly noticed Galldora on the window-sill. 'Oh, but, Mummy,' cried Marybell, 'Galldora ought to come, oughtn't she? I mean, she's a real sailor doll, and she'd be so disappointed if she didn't go to the seaside. I know she would.'

Marybell's mother sighed. 'Well, perhaps Galldora wouldn't take up much room. But don't add any more.'

'There aren't any others to take,' said Marybell happily, as she started to collect up the dolls and teddies. She had to make four journeys down to the car, and then she had to come back to the nursery, as she had forgotten Galldora.

The big dolls sat on the picnic-basket on the back seat beside Marybell, and the bigger teddy bears were propped up by the side window with the towels and bathing things to sit on, and the smaller teddies and dolls were all arranged very comfortably on the ledge at the back window.

'I am very sorry,' said Marybell's daddy, 'but you will have to take some of those bears and things away from the back window, Marybell, because I can't see out.'

So Marybell, with the help of her mother, rearranged the piles of teddies and dolls at the back. In the rearranging, Galldora got forgotten.

She was left lying on the outside step by the back
wheel.

The car started, and she went whizz out into
the air but, luckily for Galldora, her hair had
got jammed into the back door, which stopped
her from being jerked right away. She had a
most exciting ride.

It's just like flying, said Galldora to herself.
And it was. She was quite airborne, except for
her wool hair. But at the corners, and every now
and again, she went thud against the mudguard.
I wouldn't be surprised, said Galldora to her-

self, if all these walloping bangs aren't the very best thing for my stuffing. After all, it will certainly get the dust out.

It was a good thing that Uncle Jack, though he was not very good at making rag dolls, had used strong sailcloth and thick twine to make Galldora. His stitches held very well, and Galldora was really none the worse for wear when they reached the seaside, except perhaps that her hair had grown a little with all the pulling.

'Oh, my poor Galldora!' cried Marybell, when she realized what had happened, and she gathered Galldora up in her arms and took her straight away on to the sands. Galldora was sat up against the picnic-basket. She gazed out at the blue, blue sea, and the silver-gold sands, and at the sky touching the far waves, and at the white seagulls going flap, flap, flap up and down the beach.

'My!' said Galldora happily, 'this does bring back memories.' Her shoe-button eyes shone, and she hummed a sea-chanty she remembered. She hummed very, very softly, so that no one could hear; and her sea-chanty, which had a

very delightful tune, got all muddled up in the
rumbling noises of the waves as they rolled the
sand and the shells out, and then rolled them
back again.

It was a wonderful morning, really one of
the most wonderful mornings in Galldora's
life. When she wasn't humming sea-chanties
she watched all seven teddy-bears being buried
in the sand, and she waved, when no one was

looking, at the stuffed cat, who sat proudly on the top of a sand castle. The big dolls, and the new French one, Allouette, had been left in the car to sun-bathe through the window, while some of the other dolls had been dipped in the sea and taught swimming.

Nothing, thought Galldora, can go wrong with today. But she was mistaken. In the afternoon Marybell's daddy took Marybell for a sail, far out on the waves, in his rubber dinghy.

Marybell had insisted that Bobo and Galldora wanted to come. She was quite wrong, because Bobo didn't want to go – he really did hate water, it made him have a funny feeling in his whiskers.

They sailed far, far out to sea. Then, oh, dear! A dreadful thing happened. The rubber dinghy got a puncture. It must have hit a sharp rock or a sunken piece of iron, or a wreck, or something. Marybell started to cry, and Marybell's daddy, who knew all about rubber dinghies and leaks, looked very worried. Marybell's mother and the picnic-basket seemed very, very far away.

Marybell knew Bobo would be the most frightened, and so she kept on saying, 'It's all right, Bobo, it's all right.'

Marybell's daddy said nothing. He looked very grim. The water kept sloshing in, and everything got wet. Then Marybell's daddy thought of a good idea.

'Hand me the rag doll,' he said calmly. He pinched and squeezed Galldora into the leaking hole. Her head was stuck right down into the sea. 'There,' said Marybell's father cheerfully, 'that ought to get us safely back. Hang on to her legs, Marybell.' Marybell did.

Dear me, thought Galldora to herself, this is most extraordinary. There's no wind down here and no sound, and I do wish the jelly-fish would mind where they are going.

It wasn't very long before her head got muddled up with the pebbles and the shells that the surf was rolling backward and forward. One of her eyes got torn right away, and suddenly one arm got caught upon a great nail in the breakwater.

'Help!' cried Galldora. 'Help!' But no one

heard. She seemed to be tugged in all directions. Marybell was tugging at her legs, and her arm was being torn off in the other direction. Uncle Jack's stitches were strained to their utmost.

'Oh, dear! Oh, help!' cried Galldora. 'This is dreadful.' Then the rubber boat gave an extra heave, and they were on the sands.

When they pulled Galldora up she had only one eye, very little hair, and no dress left to speak of, and she was so flabby and wet that Marybell burst into tears.

Marybell's daddy picked up Galldora and wrung her out. 'She's a heroine,' he said. 'She's a brave doll. She's saved us all.'

Then he grinned, for the rag doll really did look very funny, but Galldora gasped. A heroine, she said to herself, so that's what I am, a real heroine.

Galldora was taken back to Marybell's mummy and the picnic-basket, and the whole adventure was told.

'Poor, brave Galldora,' said Marybell's mummy. 'I will certainly have to sew on a new eye and make Galldora a new dress. We can't have heroines in rags.'

'She'd better have a medal too, for life-saving,' said Marybell's daddy.

'Well, I never!' Galldora was amazed. 'They really do seem to think a lot of me.'

Galldora was given the very best place on the back window of the car as she rode home in great style. The dolls and teddies treated her with respect and admiration. 'I wouldn't be surprised if you were knighted,' said the Big Teddy in his gruff, kind voice. 'Then you would have a "Sir" before your name.'

Sir Galldora, thought Galldora to herself. Yes, that would sound very nice.

'I'm very glad it wasn't me that had to fill the hole,' said Bobo humbly, in his tiny, dry voice. 'And I think you are terribly brave, Galldora.'

Galldora smiled, she hardly heard, she was dreaming away to herself. 'Sir Galldora,' she kept on repeating softly. 'Yes, I like that very much – Sir Galldora.' And she gazed out on the passing world, with her one shining eye. 'Sir

Galldora, the great heroine – that's me, an important, lifesaving rag doll.' And she practised bowing to the passing trees and the cows, as if they were cheering crowds.

Galldora and the Woods-beyond

There was one treat that the dolls and teddy bears and the stuffed cat Bobo loved almost more than any other treat. And that was to be taken to the woods-beyond. One or two, or sometimes even three of them, were taken there when Marybell went to pick bluebells in the spring or coloured leaves in the autumn.

Now, poor Galldora was the only doll that had never been to the woods-beyond. She always pretended she didn't mind. 'Oh, woods,' Galldora would say, 'they are unkept, wild places. I much prefer gardens, where there is grass and flowers and paths all in order.'

'But you should see the woods, Galldora,' Bobo, the stuffed cat, once said. 'When the bluebells are out, Galldora, the woods look like a lake, it really does. A shining lake of blue, with the trees looking as if they were growing in the water.'

'And the birds singing,' growled the Teddy Bear softly, 'I thought it was fairies singing at first, till Marybell said they were birds.'

'Birds,' said Galldora, in a very high, trying-not-to-cry voice, 'I prefer a blackbird's song to any others. You should have heard the blackbird sing from the garden-shed this afternoon, but of course you were out.'

Then Galldora pressed her head closer to the nursery window, she did not want the Big Teddy to see that her shoe-button eyes were full of unspilt tears.

The woods-beyond, if only I could see them once, thought Galldora.

One spring night, after the dolls and teddy bears had talked even more about the woods-beyond, Galldora felt so sad she could not sleep. 'I don't care,' she kept on saying, but she did. She stayed awake and just stared out into the cool silvery garden. She stared and stared, and all the black polish on her eyes grew dim. She bumped her head so many times against the window-pane that her wool plaits frayed out and became all unplaited. Her face grew even whiter, and her sewn-on mouth seemed to turn down a little.

Next day Marybell said, 'Dolls and teddy bears, I've got a wonderful treat for you. My daddy is taking us in a car, and we are going for a picnic. Won't that be fun, my darlings?'

I wonder if she will take me too, said Galldora to herself.

Marybell put all the dolls and teddies on the floor. Then she collected them in armſuls and took them to the car. Galldora was in the last armful to be carried out and she fell, unnoticed, to the floor.

Galldora lay for some time on the nursery floor, staring at the ceiling. She heard the gay chatter and laughter in the hall as the picnic party collected. She heard Marybell's daddy starting up the car in the garage. She heard the car back round to the front door. She heard them all climb in, and then she heard the car door slam. She heard the car start on its way. She heard it hoot at the end of the drive. She heard the car purr into the distance, and for a long time after that she continued lying on the floor, staring at the ceiling.

'I don't think I can bear to hear them all talking of the picnic. They'll tell me all about it, every bit of it, and it will make me more and more sad.'

Suddenly the nursery door was pushed slowly open. Galldora stayed very still. Sparks, the spaniel dog, came and sniffed her. Galldora kept very silent. Then Sparks patted her with his paw. Galldora was so flabby that when the dog patted her she jumped, and this amused Sparks. He wagged his tail. He patted her again. Galldora leaped into the air, and fell with a soft *plop*. Then Sparks closed his teeth very softly and gently round Galldora, and he ran with her from the room, wagging his tail delightedly.

He trotted down the stairs with Galldora in his mouth. He went into the garden and put Galldora down on the lawn. He looked at her. Then he pushed her around with his nose again and patted her up into the air with his paws.

The cook flung open the kitchen window and

shouted, 'What have you got there, Sparks?
Put it down at once, you naughty dog.'

Sparks looked round in a guilty way. He
quickly picked Galldora up again, with a gentle
mouth, for he was really a good dog, and ran
out of the garden, into the field, and on to the
woods.

Once in the woods, Sparks put Galldora down
very gently on to a bed of moss against a tree.
Sparks sniffed the sweet air. Rabbits, he sniffed.
He was soon barking joyfully at the rabbit-
holes. Then running and jumping at the rustles
in the tangles of briar and weeds, here, then
there, then farther on. Galldora looked about
her. 'The wood – this must be the woods-
beyond.' There was magic in the very thought.
All about the wood was a strange light, a blue
sheen of light.

At first Galldora could not think where the light came from. Then she noticed it came as if from the bluebells, which were flowering and moving gently in the breeze, like waves on a shining sheet of blue water. Near her was a clump of late primroses. Butterflies flittered in twos and threes, joyfully, looking like flowers as they fluttered. The branches made a canopy of pale green, and the pussy-willow and the last of the catkins were like signposts to the sunshine.

Over all, and above the chatter of the rooks, came the ringing, bell-like call of a great tit and the flute of a robin and the softly trickling song of the willow warbler.

The birds singing in the woods-beyond, I have heard them, I have heard them, said Galldora to herself, and gave a long, happy sigh.

After seeking rabbits and finding none Sparks went home and forgot about the rag doll. But Galldora didn't even notice, she was so happy.

The rain came and pattered down on to Galldora's woolly head. The moon came out and

glinted on Galldora's black shoe-button eyes. Then the dawn broke and set a soft glow stealing over Galldora's white rag face. All the time Galldora kept saying: 'I am in the woods-beyond, I am in the woods-beyond.' After two nights and two days Galldora was still in a dream of happiness, sitting on her soft cushion of moss, propped against the tree, with the robins chirping about her and the butterflies sometimes resting on her rag hand.

None of the other dolls and none of the teddies or even Bobo, the stuffed cat, have been in the wood at night, thought Galldora. But I have.

After three days Marybell came up to the woods to pick bluebells, and she brought Sparks. Sparks suddenly remembered Galldora. He dashed here and there and sniffed her out. He took her up and worried her, growling in a friendly way.

'Sparks – here – good dog!' called Marybell. 'Here, Sparks, what have you found?' Sparks bounded up to his mistress with Galldora hanging limply from his mouth. 'Why!' gasped Marybell, 'it's my very own rag doll!' She gazed at Galldora in a motherly way and shook her head sadly. 'Poor old thing,' she said, 'poor old, silly old thing, you are in a mess. Wet through and so dirty. I'll have to dry you out by the fire, and sew a new dress on you. Come on, let's get you home at once, or you'll catch a dreadful cold.' Galldora was carried home and seated in the best place against the nursery fender.

'We've been for three picnics now, Galldora,' said Bobo. Galldora smiled.

'Up on the downs. Oh, you should see the downs, Galldora,' growled the Big Teddy. 'They are my favourite place.' Galldora just smiled.

'Oh, you should go in a car some time, Galldora,' said Lulu. Galldora hardly listened. She was so happy, and still dreaming of the magic of the woods-beyond.

'What a pity you haven't seen the stream where we picnic, but perhaps next time,' said Little White Teddy Bear to Galldora, as kindly as he could.

'The woods-beyond,' sighed Galldora in a dreamy way.

'Magic,' said Galldora, still in a dream. 'At night,' said Galldora, hardly above a whisper. 'At night.'

The teddy bears were silent, and the dolls looked at each other. Then Galldora told them all about it.

'How brave you are, Galldora,' said Bobo,

'to have been in the woods-beyond at night all by yourself.'

'Oh! the moonlight and the owls,' murmured Galldora. 'It's magic! Oh, yes! It's the best place of all – the woods-beyond at night.'

Galldora and the Rabbit Pie

'I do so want a rabbit,' said Marybell. The rabbit she wanted was a small black and white one, and the rabbit was owned by a boy called Tony. 'Oh, please,' begged Marybell, holding the rabbit very tightly, 'please, Tony, won't you give him to me?'

'No,' said Tony firmly, 'and you're squeezing it, Marybell. Give him back.' Marybell handed back the small rabbit.

The rabbit's mother was peeping out of the open door of her hutch, very anxiously. She knew one of her eight babies was out and she waffled her nose and pricked her ears. Tony put the baby rabbit back, closed the hutch, and went on cleaning up the yard. He took no more notice of Marybell. Marybell, very sadly, went out of Tony's garden. She stopped for just a brief moment at the gate and looked at the notice again. She couldn't read very well, but she knew it said:

LOTS OF RABBITS FOR SALE. TWO AND SIX-PENCE EACH. APPLY TONY ACKROYD, THE WILLOWS, QUEXON HILL, MERRYFIELDS. TELEPHONE NUMBER, MERRYFIELDS 246.

'I think he's a jolly mean, stinky little boy.' said Marybell furiously, after she had looked at the notice, and she went home, walking in her special strutty way that made her plaid skirt swirl.

'Can I have two shillings and sixpence?' Marybell asked her Mummy at lunch.

'Certainly not!' answered Marybell's mother.

'Money's getting very expensive,' said Marybell, 'and three pennies a week doesn't last out.'

'It's quite enough for a little girl,' answered Marybell's mother firmly.

When Marybell's daddy came back from work Marybell said, 'Please, Daddy, can I have two shillings and sixpence?'

'Now, you know, Marybell,' said Marybell's

daddy, 'we said three pennies a week and no more, didn't we?'

'But I want it for something very special,' said Marybell seriously. Marybell's daddy was not in a very talkative mood. He wasn't really listening to Marybell; he was thinking of other things.

'I can't tell you what it is,' went on Marybell, 'for it's a secret, but I want it for a very, very, very special reason.'

'Isn't it your bedtime yet?' said Marybell's father. Marybell gave a big sigh. It was clearly going to be no good asking her daddy for two shillings and sixpence.

When Marybell was in bed and before she went to sleep she had a long, deep think about the two and sixpence and the rabbit. It was such a dear little thing, so small and furry, and so very soft. It had such very black ears and such very black paws and such queer black dots and dashes down its back. Its eyes were blue, not red, which Marybell thought was much more attractive. Some of the other babies had brown markings and some were almost quite white.

Some had pointed faces, but this one – the one that Marybell really wanted – had a broad, flat face. 'It's got to be mine,' said Marybell before she went to sleep. 'It's simply got to be mine.'

When Marybell woke up it was very early. She always woke up very early, and there was a long long wait before Marybell's mummy and daddy got up. Marybell at once thought about the rabbit. She dressed herself, and went out of the house and down the road. She went to Quexon Hill and into Tony's garden. She opened the rabbit-hutch and looked at the babies. She put her hand into the bundle of babies and found the black-nosed rabbit, and took it out and cuddled it.

'Hi,' called a voice, 'put that rabbit back!' Marybell looked round. There was Tony stand-watching her.

'I want it,' said Marybell.

'Where's your two and six?' said Tony, quite unmoved. Marybell was a little frightened of Tony. Tony was a whole four years older than Marybell.

'I haven't got two and six,' said Marybell,

putting on her baby voice, 'but I want the baby
rabbit, please, Tony.'

'Well, you can't have it,' answered Tony.
'Put it back at once.' If Tony had been a
grown-up Marybell's baby voice would have
had results. It nearly always did, but Tony
wasn't grown-up, and Tony was quite unmoved. He stood there in his khaki shorts and
striped jersey, with his hair very much on end,
hands in his pockets, and just stared. Marybell

knew she had to do as he said. So she put the rabbit back. She closed the door of the hutch. She stood sucking her thumb. 'Go home,' ordered Tony, 'your mother will be missing you.'

'She isn't up yet,' said Marybell. It was a lovely morning, cool and sunny, with the promise of great heat later on. The bees were thick in the catmint and the lavender. The roses, washed with the night dew, looked shining and clear. The white pigeons were cooing on the dovecote, and a young blackbird was pecking at a strawberry through the net in the silent kitchen garden.

'Why can't I have the baby rabbit?' asked Marybell, pouting.

'Because you haven't got two and six,' said Tony, keeping his eyes very round and unblinking.

'I'll give you a sucky sweet,' said Marybell hopefully.

'I don't want one,' said Tony.

'I'll get three pennies for my pocket money tomorrow,' said Marybell. 'You can have that.'

'Three pennies are not enough,' answered Tony, still standing very solidly and squarely in the path.

'Well, I've got seven farthings saved up,' went on Marybell.

'That's only a penny and three farthings,' said Tony.

'But I can't get two whole shillings,' said Marybell drooping her lip.

'Two shillings and sixpence,' corrected Tony.

'I can't get it, I tell you,' said Marybell. 'Mummy won't give it to me, and my daddy won't give it to me.'

'Well, then, you can't have the rabbit,' answered Tony.

'But how do you get money?' asked Marybell, almost in tears. She did so want the rabbit.

'You have to work to get money,' said Tony. 'I clean out my rabbits, and go out and collect dandelions and grass, and I have to go to the farm and ask for the straw and collect it. There's a lot of work in keeping rabbits. Why don't you go home and work?' Marybell's eyes began to swim with tears.

'I'm a very little girl,' she said.

'You're not as little as my baby sister,' said Tony. 'How old are you?'

'I'm not going to tell you,' answered Marybell crossly.

'My baby sister is two,' said Tony. There didn't seem to be any answer to that, so Marybell went back to her home and her breakfast very sadly.

Nobody seemed to notice that Marybell was a very sad girl. Everybody in the house was extra busy. They were busy because a visitor was coming to dinner. The visitor was a captain. The captain was so important that there was extra cleaning and dusting and cooking to be done. There were flowers to be arranged and, oh, all sorts of things to be done, and nobody was at all interested in Marybell.

She went up to her nursery and looked at all her dolls and didn't want to play with any of them. She looked at her teddies, and they all seemed very dull compared to the baby rabbit. She went to the nursery window, and on the window-sill was her old rag doll, Galldora. Inside Galldora were the seven farthings. They were kept there for safe-keeping. Marybell took up Galldora and went back to Tony. She found Tony in a garden-shed, playing with his train.

'I've brought you my rag doll,' said Marybell.

'What for?' asked Tony.

'She's got seven farthings sewn up inside her,' said Marybell. 'I keep them there for safe-keeping. You can have Galldora and the farthings if I can have the rabbit.'

'But I don't like dolls,' said Tony, without looking up. 'I like trains and soldiers. Haven't you got any soldiers?'

'No,' said Marybell, 'but Galldora's a very nice rag doll, though she is a bit flabby now. She's as old as I am.' Tony looked at Galldora. He took her and examined her. She had shoe-button eyes. Well, he thought, the shoe buttons might come in useful. She had wool hair, but the wool was too weak for tying up anything; and she had a dress which could be cut off and might come in useful for polishing his trains, but it wasn't a very long dress.

'She's not worth much,' said Tony, handing her back.

'Would you like one of my teddies?' asked Marybell hopefully.

'I've got my own teddy, and I don't want another,' said Tony. 'And I think dolls are silly things. The only fun you can have with dolls is cutting off their hair. Haven't you got a train?' Marybell shook her head. 'Oh, well,' said Tony, 'you'll have to get two shillings and sixpence.'

'Can I go and just hold the baby rabbit for a little while, please?' begged Marybell.

'No,' said Tony. 'you'll only upset the mother.' Marybell started to cry. Tony watched her. He was very much alarmed. He didn't like girls crying and he always got into trouble when his baby sister cried. 'I'll tell you what,' he said, 'you can have the rabbit for a shilling.'

'Oh, can I really?' said Marybell, cheering up.

'Yes,' said Tony, 'that's letting you off a whole shilling and sixpence, and it means I can't get as many soldiers as I'd planned to. Still, you can have the rabbit for a shilling.'

After the first moment of joy Marybell was suddenly downcast again. 'But where am I to get a shilling from?' she asked.

'Go home and help your mummy,' said Tony, 'and she'll give you a shilling.' Marybell went happily home. She was quite certain that Tony knew about everything and all she had to do now was to help her mummy.

The hours were passing and still nothing was ready for the visit of the captain. Marybell's mother was to-ing and fro-ing from room to room.

'Can I help you, mummy?' asked Marybell.

'No, dear, not now,' answered Marybell's mother absent-mindedly, and went on talking out loud, but really to herself, 'Oh, dear! We really do need another vase of flowers over in that corner. It does look very dull without them, and the captain is a great gardener, so I think roses. Robert, dear, could I pick some more roses?'

Marybell's daddy, in rolled-up shirt sleeves and with a worried frown on his face, said 'Oh, Mary! Do you really have to have any more roses? There won't be any left in the garden, and the captain is an expert on roses and I did so want –'

'All right, Robert, I'll get some syringa.'

'Daddy,' asked Marybell, following her daddy into the garden, 'can I help you?'

'No, Marybell, not today. Now, where did I put the spanner. I'll never get the lawn cut in time. Well? What is it, Marybell?'

'I want to help you, Daddy.'

'Look, Marybell, dear, just run away and play, can't you? There's a good girl.'

Marybell stood on the lawn, holding Galldora by the leg and swinging her up and down. Marybell was thinking deeply. Then she went into the kitchen. On the kitchen-table was a milk bottle, a rolling-pin, and some pastry left on a marble slab, for Marybell's mother was wonderful at making puff pastry. There was an earthenware dish with some cooked rabbit and gravy. Marybell propped Galldora up against the milk bottle and stood staring at the table, thinking. She wondered if she dare roll out the pastry. Would her mother be pleased, or very

cross? She decided her mother would be very cross. The kitchen was cool and neat, and all the washing up had been done. In the basket was Sparks, the spaniel, and everything was in order.

Perhaps I could help by making tea, thought Marybell. So she lifted down the electric kettle and filled it with water from the tap at the sink by standing on a chair. It was rather heavy and, struggling back with it, she knocked the table. The pie-dish started to wobble. Marybell's mother had left it far too near the edge. It wobbled for a long time while Marybell stood still, watching it. She had the kettle in her hand and couldn't think how to manage the kettle and stop the dish wobbling.

Sparks too was greatly interested in the wobbling dish. He watched it with his spaniel ears pricked as far as a spaniel's ears could be pricked. Then, with a *splosh*, the dish fell onto the linoleum floor. Sparks was now very interested. While Marybell put the kettle on to the table near the cooker Sparks had left his basket and gobbled and gobbled up most of the rabbit.

'Naughty Sparks!' scolded Marybell. She put back the two small bits of rabbit that were left and as much of the vegetables as she could scoop up with a spoon, and as much of the gravy as she could, then she mopped up the rest with the dish-cloth and squeezed it into the pie. She was thankful the dish hadn't broken. But Marybell was worried. The dish did look very empty now, and if her mummy knew what had happened she would never get her shilling.

Then Marybell's eyes fell on Galldora. She picked Galldora up and pushed her into the pie-dish. The pie-dish looked almost full, with Galldora squeezed down and the two bits of rabbit, the vegetables, and the gravy on top.

Help! thought Galldora. Help!

Just then Marybell's mother came into the kitchen and, as she was in a terrible fluster because the captain had arrived an hour earlier than he was expected, she didn't look closely at the pie. She rolled out the pastry and popped it on to the top of Galldora and the gravy.

Oh, dear me! thought Galldora. Now what?

Galldora didn't have to wonder long, for she was lifted up in the pie-dish and put into a hot oven.

This is terrible, said Galldora to herself. This is terrible. I don't like this a bit. It's all dark and stuffy, and the gravy is all getting into my hair.

The pie-dish grew hotter and hotter, and Galldora grew more and more nervous.

I am sure I shall just disappear, she kept thinking, and then there won't be any ME left.

Marybell's mother, having put the pie into the oven, had dashed upstairs to change her dress and brush her hair. Marybell's daddy had taken the captain into the garden to show him the roses.

Marybell was left standing in the kitchen, nervously wondering if her rag doll was all right.

She felt very sorry for Galldora and hadn't realized, not really, that Galldora would have to go into the oven. Marybell was so upset that she got into Sparks' basket and cuddled up with him.

Marybell's mother came into the kitchen, saw Marybell, and said: 'Oh, Marybell, really! You are being most irritating to-day. Just look at you! All covered with dog's hairs.'

Marybell was dragged upstairs, scrubbed and washed, and her hair brushed and brushed, and she was put into her best blue dress, with blue ribbons in her hair; and her socks were changed for her very best white socks, and her shoes for her best white sandals. Then she was taken down to the drawing-room.

'Aha,' said the captain, 'so here's the little girl.'

'Do you like rabbits?' asked Marybell at once, hoping that the captain might say Yes and buy her the baby rabbit from Tony.

'The captain simply loves rabbit, don't you Captain?' said Marybell's daddy.

'What, what?' said the captain, puffing a

little through his very fine and well-trimmed moustache.

'My wife always remembers that you love rabbit pie, don't you, Mary?'

Marybell's mother smiled and said, 'Yes, I always remember.'

The captain spluttered a little. 'Excellent, excellent!' he said at last. Marybell, watching, didn't miss a single expression on the captain's face.

'You know, Marybell,' explained Marybell's daddy, 'the first time the captain came to lunch, your mother gave him one of her rabbit pies, and he said rabbit pie was his favourite meal.'

'Did he?' said Marybell. But she wasn't at all sure that he did, because, for just a second, the captain had that sort of face on, that she herself put on, when she had to eat cornflour pudding, which she simply hated.

At last lunch was ready. After the soup in came the rabbit pie. Marybell was feeling very nervous and fidgety. She wondered what they'd say about Galldora.

'I think it's awfully cruel to eat rabbits,' she

said. No one took any notice of her remark, and Marybell's daddy cut the puff pastry and then tried to get out a piece of rabbit. He found it very difficult. Marybell was feeling very, very nervous. 'I think it's awfully cruel to eat rabbits,' she said louder. Marybell's mother was looking anxious and the captain was pretending not to notice, and Marybell's daddy was having a very difficult time indeed. At last he got the fork all twisted up in Galldora's hair and, with a *plop*, out came Galldora's head. Marybell's mother screamed, and Marybell's daddy gasped, 'What on earth . . .?' He was staring down at two shoe-button eyes. 'I think it's awfully cruel to eat rabbits,' said Marybell, as loudly as she could.

'Why, it's Galldora!' said Marybell's daddy, as he pulled out a long, weak-looking rag doll.

'Marybell! Oh, you bad girl!' sobbed Marybell's mother.

'I think it's awfully cruel to eat rabbits,' said Marybell stubbornly. The captain burst into laughter.

'Quite right, my dear, quite right. You stick

to your idea. You thought it was cruel to eat rabbit, so you gave us your doll to eat instead. Was that it?'

Marybell, at last finding somebody listening to her, said very quickly and all at oncc, 'I was helping because I wanted a shilling to buy one of Tony's baby rabbits – the black and white one. Oh, it's ever so sweet. He's got eight and he said I could have one for a shilling, and he said my mummy would give me a shilling if I helped her, so I did try to help, but it all went wrong. Oh, it is such a sweet baby rabbit!'

The captain gave Marybell a shilling and said, 'There, that's for the baby rabbit.' He seemed in very good spirits and said he enjoyed eating just potatoes and butter; he liked nothing better.

After lunch the captain decided to go with Marybell to get the rabbit. He told Marybell as they walked down the road together that he was delighted that Galldora was in the pie, for if there was one thing he really hated eating it was rabbit pie; but he asked Marybell to keep it a great secret, as he didn't want to hurt her mum-

my's feelings. Marybell quite understood, and was very pleased to keep the secret.

And Galldora – well, after a good wash, Galldora was pegged on to the line and left to dry. She really didn't look any the worse for her rough treatment. She hung there, proudly telling all the bees and butterflies that flew about her, 'I saved the whole situation by being baked in a pie.'

Galldora and the Mermaid

One day Galldora was given a new dress and taken by Marybell to the seaside for a holiday.

'What a strange doll,' said the landlady, Mrs Cockle, when she saw Galldora.

'She's not really strange,' answered Marybell, 'she's just a rag doll.' Marybell spoke as stiffly as she could, because she was upset that the landlady was so rude about Galldora.

'Yes, my dear, I can see she is a rag doll,' said the landlady slowly, 'but she's strange all the same. She's very faded and flabby, poor thing, but perhaps the sea air will do her good. Let's hope so.'

'It's just her new dress that makes her look washed out,' explained Marybell, talking very fast to get in all she wanted to say. 'It is rather a bright colour. It's a piece of Mummy's worn-out dance dress. Mummy calls it flame colour. I'm not sure I like that colour myself. Blue's my

favourite colour, that's why I bought a blue
ribbon for Galldora's hair. I spent a whole four-
pence on that ribbon. The colour's called king-
fisher blue, and it doesn't look quite right with
flame colour, but it is pretty all the same.'

'Very pretty,' Mrs Cockle said, adding, 'It's a
pity about the safety-pin though, it's so large
that it hides most of the ribbon.'

'Well, but, you see, Mrs Cockle, I had to pin
it on Galldora's hair, because Galldora can't
keep ribbons on her hair. It's wool hair, Mrs
Cockle, and it's got a bit moth-eaten, and her

head's such a funny shape too, sort of flattish, do you see what I mean?'

Galldora was held up for inspection. Mrs Cockle inspected Galldora's head. 'Yes, very flat, my dear, and a very odd shape.'

Now, Galldora was not at all pleased at this conversation. She loved being looked at, but she felt it was very rude indeed of people to make remarks on the shape of her head.

Human beings, she thought to herself, have no manners, no manners at all. Certainly none where dolls are concerned.

I think the discussion on Galldora's head would have spoilt the whole of Galldora's holiday if it hadn't been for an adventure that came her way on the first evening.

It was a wonderful adventure, and Galldora was able to tell all the other dolls and the teddy bears about it when she returned to the nursery. It happened like this. Marybell was so eager to rush down to the sands and the sea at once that her mother promised to take her down as soon as they had unpacked the spade, the bucket, and the swimsuits.

'We won't wait for lunch,' said Marybell's mother, 'we'll ask Mrs Cockle if she could make us some sandwiches and we'll eat them on the sands.'

Mrs Cockle understood all about little girls wanting to rush on to the sands and not waste a moment so she bustled about and produced a packed lunch.

'There you are, my dear,' she said to Marybell's mother, as she handed over the lunch, and turning to Marybell she added, 'That's right, love, you take that doll down and give her a good sea blow, that will do the poor thing a power of good.'

The sands and the sea were all that sands and sea should be. The sands were silver white, stretching as far to the right and as far to the left as Marybell could see, and the great ocean was in a very gentle mood.

'Oh, Mummy,' said Marybell, 'I want to stay here always and always.'

'Well, we have till six o'clock,' answered Marybell's mother. 'Now, how about a paddle, Marybell, while I get the lunch set out? Then after lunch I'll help you build a sand castle, and later we will go and have a real swim.'

So after their lunch Marybell's mother helped Marybell to build the hugest and the most magnificent sand castle that Galldora had cvcr sccn. It was so large that Marybell could stand in the middle courtyard without knocking any of the castle walls down. The castle had turrets and windows, and a moat, and a wall round the moat, with more turrets and more windows. When the castle was finished Galldora was sat on a sand-throne made especially for her. She sat there happily and proudly staring out over the castle walls.

After a swim Marybell decided to look for shells. She and her mother were so happy collecting shells and shining wet pebbles that Marybell's mother forgot all about the time. When she did look at her watch she was horrified.

'Quickly, Marybell,' she said, 'we mustn't be late the very first day. Mrs Cockle said she would have a high tea waiting for us at six, and it is six o'clock now.'

There was a lot of collecting up to be done. Wet towels and bathing-suits were crammed into one basket. Then into another basket went the paper wrappings of the lunch and the sun-hats and the sun-glasses, while in the bucket went the pebbles and shells. With all the pushing of this here and that there, both Marybell and Marybell's mother forgot Galldora. Marybell's mother did say, 'Have you got Galldora, Marybell?' and Marybell had answered, 'Yes, Mummy, I put her with my swim-suit.' And Marybell really thought she had. Galldora couldn't be seen, for the sand-throne she had been sitting on had collapsed, and she had sunk forward against the wall. She was still upright, and her head rested against a turret, but she was hidden and she couldn't see anything but sand. Galldora heard Marybell chattering as she and her mother hurried away from the beach, back to Mrs Cockle and high tea. Soon the beach grew very quiet except for the wild noises of sea-birds. Then the noise of the sea seemed to grow louder.

The half-hours went by, and the sky changed

from blue to a flush of pink and yellow gold. If only Galldora could have seen how wonderful the sky was, for it looked as if some giant child of the sky-lands had tipped up a basket full of rose petals and set them floating down. Then the colour left the sky, and a silver bloom lingered on all the sea and the sands. All the while the sound of the sea grew louder.

I know I'm not fancying it, said Galldora to herself. It's true, the sea is coming towards me inch by inch.

It was true. The tide was rolling in the white surf, and with the incoming tide a low wind had sprung up. The wind stirred the white sand and set the white horses riding far out at sea. It may have been the dragging of the sands, as the sea washed out before each incoming wave swept up, or it may have been the low wind shifting the sands, but whatever was the cause, the walls of the castle cracked and slowly, very slowly, crumbled.

'Gracious me,' gasped Galldora, 'I can see now – and how very different everything looks. Mrs Cockle wouldn't approve at all. Why everything looks as pale and as washed-out as my face.'

The silver bloom about the scene turned clearer and harder. Shadows sprung like seaweed in a silver wash. All in the dark and the light of the waves were a million phosphorous sea life, that glowed so gaily it looked as if the fish were holding a great ball, far down below. The moon, like a full-sailed ship riding high, seemed to let drift a fishing-net of light to glitter and shimmer on the sea.

It's very beautiful, thought Galldora, but I rather wish I wasn't here. I think Mrs Cockle's boarding-house would be more cosy. Still, it's no good me wishing, as here I am and here I'll have to stay until Marybell finds me tomorrow.

All the time the sea crept closer, wave by wave. This began to worry Galldora.

I wish the sea would stop – just stop where it is, thought Galldora. If it doesn't my castle will soon be washed away and I with it. And then she sighed, 'Oh, dear, poor Marybell, she won't have a rag doll any more.'

Just then Galldora thought she heard sweet

singing. I've got myself into such a state of nerves, I'm imagining all sorts of things, she told herself crossly. Why, that's only the noise of the sea or the wind or a bird. But try as Galldora would to make herself believe the singing noise was just natural noises, she couldn't. The singing grew louder and higher. I don't think I like that singing at all, thought Galldora, it makes me feel uncomfortable.

Then Galldora noticed a shape on one of the white horses far out in the sea. As the shape came nearer Galldora thought it was a girl. A girl with long, shining hair. And it was a girl. The girl was singing.

Nearer and nearer came the white horse and the girl with the long hair, until with a sudden *splosh*, she was washed up on shore. Then Galldora saw she was not a proper girl, but a mermaid.

The mermaid was in a shocking temper. She clearly hated being on the shore. She stopped singing and lashed her tail, and was very thankful when the next wave lifted her up and washed her out into the sea again.

'Oh, do stop and talk to me, please?' called Galldora. 'I've never talked to a mermaid before. But perhaps you can't talk.'

'Of course I can, silly,' answered the mermaid. 'But where are you?'

'In here,' called Galldora, 'Here in the sand castle.' The mermaid swam close to the shore to have a look.

'I can't see with all this hair,' said the mermaid at last, and she tossed her hair this way and that.

'I'm just near you,' explained Galldora, 'for the sea has come up to my castle walls, and I'm terribly afraid it will wash it and me away.'

The mermaid lifted up her silvery hair with her two hands. 'That's better,' she said. 'Ah, yes, I can see you now. My, aren't you small, and you haven't got much hair – how very strange.'

'Oh, yes, I know all about that,' said poor Galldora. 'And I've got a funny-shaped head, but I'm used to it, and it's *my* hair and *my* head, and, anyway, talking of hair, you've got far too much. You ought to have it cut off.'

'Cut it off – how do you do that?' asked the mermaid. Then Galldora realized at once she had made a very silly remark, because, of course, who would have scissors in the sea. 'Oh, I've changed my mind,' she said hurriedly, 'I shouldn't cut your hair off if I were you; it suits you.'

'If you had to choose between one eye and three eyes,' said the mermaid, 'which would you choose?'

'I've often had one eye,' said Galldora, 'and another one can always be sewn on, but three would look ugly, very ugly indeed. So I would choose one.'

'I'd choose three,' said the mermaid, 'a third one in the middle of my forehead, then when I opened my middle eye, the lashes would lift my hair a little, so I could see. It's a dreadful nuisance not being able to see properly. Look what happened just now. I got washed ashore, just because I couldn't see where I was going.'

'Yes, I do understand what you mean,' said Galldora thoughtfully.

'Can't you think of something to help me?' asked the mermaid.

'I'll try,' said Galldora. 'You can see now, though, can't you?'

'Yes, because I'm lifting my hair with my hands, but it gets trying.'

'Of course,' said Galldora. Then she asked, 'Do other mermaids have this trouble?'

'No,' answered the mermaid. 'It's because I'm a bad mermaid I have this trouble. The good mermaids sit on rocks and sing to the sailors, and it makes the sailors muddled and then they wreck their ships on the rocks. The

ships sink, and the mermaids go swimming down and down into the wrecks and they find all sorts of treasures, like string and mirrors and combs. The mermaids make their hair behave by combing it, then they tie it up with the string, and then they look at themselves in the mirrors.'

'Just a moment,' said Galldora. 'I'm getting a bit muddled, or are you? Surely if mermaids wreck ships that's being very wicked and bad.'

'No, that's being good.' said the mermaid. 'Being bad is being like me, not wrecking ships, but just playing about in the sea. Oh, I love playing!'

'I think I'll have to think this out,' muttered Galldora, feeling very muddled.

Just then a crab who had been silently listening started to laugh and said, 'What a joke – thinking.'

'It's all very well for you to laugh,' said Galldora crossly, 'but you don't have to think this out like I do. You understand the sea and sea-creatures. I don't.'

'Don't try,' answered the crab. 'Some folks do things sideways, like me, some folks do things flat ways, like plaice, while other folks do things along, like eels do. But mermaids, they do things upside down.'

'Yes,' Galldora had a long think. 'That's very helpful,' she said. 'Thank you, Mr Crab, for telling me. I understand now. Being good is being bad to mermaids and being bad is being good, is that it?'

'It is and it isn't,' answered the crab, 'it just depends. Now, for instance, mermaids take a lot of trouble to save sailors' lives, after wrecking their ships. You can't reason with mermaids, it's better to give them a "hello", in passing and let them be. Don't have no conversation with mermaids and above all don't listen to them singing. It will muddle you.'

'Thank you,' said Galldora, 'thank you very much, Mr Crab.'

'You're welcome,' mumbled the crab, as he walked away sideways.

'That was very kind of him,' said Galldora out loud.

'Oh, was it?' snapped the mermaid. 'I think it was most spiteful of that crab and he was just talking rubbish. Oh, do hurry up and think of something to keep the hair out of my eyes, my arms are aching, and I want to go and play!'

'I know,' said Galldora, 'I've got the very thing for you – my ribbon.'

'Give it to me,' said the mermaid, putting out a hand and letting half of her long hair fall down.

'Well, I can't exactly give it to you,' answered Galldora sadly, 'you will have to come and get it. I'm a doll, you see, and I can't walk.'

The mermaid swam about on the edge of the waves and peered at the rag doll, and got very cross. She pouted and flicked her tail and then said, 'I can't walk either, so we'll just have to wait for the sea to come up and wash you to me, that's all.'

'Oh, I do hope not, what will become of me then?' gasped Galldora.

'Don't you like the sea?' asked the mermaid in surprise.

'No.'

'That's funny, the sea is safe.'

'Yes, to you, because you are a mermaid, but I'm a rag doll, and rag dolls find the sea very unsafe, I can assure you.'

'What colour is your ribbon?' asked the mermaid, changing the subject.

'Blue,' said Galldora.

'I like blue,' said the mermaid.

'It's got a silver safety-pin holding the ribbon to my hair.'

'What's a safety-pin like? I can't see.'

'You've let your hair go all over your face again, that's why,' said Galldora.

'Well, my arms were aching so,' answered the mermaid. 'Oh, I do wish the sea would hurry up and wash you out!'

'Do you think it really will?' gasped Galldora in alarm.

'Oh, yes, of course,' answered the mermaid, 'I know it will. It's still coming in, and your castle wall is slowly crumbling.'

'If I am a good rag doll –' began Galldora, then she stopped. 'Of course,' she mumbled to herself, 'it's the other way round with mermaids.' So she started again. 'If I am a bad rag doll and let you have my ribbon for keeps and my safety-pin, will you be a bad mermaid in return and throw me out of the sea far behind the castle, where I will be safe.'

'Oh, yes, all right,' said the mermaid, 'let's be bad together,' which, of course, to the mermaid meant being good.

So when at last the sea broke through the castle walls and washed Galldora out the mermaid picked her up. The mermaid took her blue ribbon and the safety-pin, and then threw her over the crumbling castle on to the far dry sand.

'Thank you,' shouted Galldora, lying on her back in the sand-dunes. 'Does the ribbon work?' she called.

'Yes, rather,' shouted back the mermaid, 'I've tied some of my hair one side with the ribbon and pulled some of the other through the safety-pin. It's lovely. I can see now. I can go and play and play and play. I'll be able to play catch with the porpoises like I never did before, and grandmother's steps with the whales. What fun!'

Then, as the mermaid swam away singing, she turned just for a second and waved a last good-bye to the rag doll. Soon her song was lost in the song of the sea, and the silver flick of her silver tail was lost in the silver of the moon's light that spread upon the waters.

Galldora was found next day by Marybell, and Marybell knew at once that she must have had some strange adventure, for how else did the rag doll leave the sea-washed castle, and how did she lose her ribbon and the safety-pin?

'I hope it was happy adventure,' said Marybell to Galldora. Galldora's shoe-button eyes shone back so brightly that Marybell knew it had indeed been a very happy adventure, and she was glad.

Galldora and the Rooks

One wild, windy day Galldora, the rag doll, was swung up into the air by Marybell. Up and up the wind carried Galldora, but she never came down, for Galldora fell *plomp* into an old rooks' nest. It was a thin old nest full of holes, and the rag doll settled right in the middle. Galldora looked down, and far below she saw the grass like a green sea, and Marybell far, far away.

'Oh!' said Galldora to herself. 'Now what will become of me?'

'Never mind, Galldora,' called up Marybell, 'the twigs will soon break in this wind and you'll come falling down. I'll go away and have my tea now and come back for you later.'

But Marybell forgot to come back. Anyway it would have been no good, for the twigs held and Galldora remained stuck in the old rooks' nest.

Next day two rooks came and looked at the rag doll.

'Aaaah!' said one.

'Aaaah!' said the other.

'Oh, go away, rooks,' said Galldora. 'Don't bother me. This is my home now and I'm happy here.'

But the two rooks started pulling Galldora about. One pulled her arms while the other pulled her feet. But as they were both pulling in different ways, Galldora stayed where she was.

At last the rooks gave up. They hopped from branch to branch, flapping their wings and looking again at the rag doll. They looked at her this way, then they looked at her that way. Then one rook looked at her from above, and the other rook looked at her from below.

One rook called, 'Floor.'

'Aaaah!' called the other, nodding its head. 'Floor-floor.'

They flew away, still calling 'Floor-floor' to each other.

What do they mean? Galldora asked herself. She soon found out. They made her into a floor and built a new nest on top of her. After a few

days she was covered with twigs, and only her head stuck up in the middle.

After a few more days there were five eggs in the nest. The mother rook sat on the eggs to keep them warm. When she flew off to find food Galldora kept the eggs warm with her wool hair.

One sunny day out of the five eggs, with a peck-peck, came five baby rooks.

'Aaaah! Aren't my babies bonny?' called the mother rook proudly.

If I was asked, said Galldora to herself, I would say I had never seen such ugly babies.

But though Galldora thought they were ugly, she took a great liking to the baby rooks, and she began to feel motherly towards them. At first she did not like the way they pecked her eyes and pulled at her hair, but she got used to it.

Then, after a while, the baby rooks grew so big that the nest seemed very crowded and much too small.

'I do wish they wouldn't sit on my head,' said poor Galldora.

One night the wind started to blow. It blew in a wild way, and it bent and shook the high tree and the rooks' nest. The father and mother rook became very worried. They kept calling 'Aaaah-aaaah!' to each other.

Whatever happens, said Galldora to herself, very firmly, I must not fall down, for if I fall the nest will come down too, and then what will happen to the baby rooks? And yet, added Galldora sadly, I would like to fall down. I am getting very tired of being up here. The baby rooks have grown so big, and the nest is getting very stuffy. Still, I must not be selfish and think about myself.

As the wind blew out the night stars and then blew in the dawn the rag doll began to feel very strange. Her legs had fallen down and only her arms held up the nest.

'Listen, baby rooks,' she said. 'Sit on my arms and head, so that when I fall down you can float down with me.'

The baby rooks did as Galldora said. With the last wild gust of wind Galldora fell, and the baby rooks, sitting on her, floated down. They fell on a soft flower-bed, Galldora first and the baby rooks on top of her.

The mother rook and father rook were so happy that their babies were safe, they gave

Galldora a couple of sharp pecks with their beaks and said, 'Aaah-aah!' in a thank you way.

The baby rooks were calling, 'We can fly.' And they started right away flapping their wings, and taking little flops from here to there. Soon they were all safe on a low May-tree.

Later Marybell found Galldora. She gave her a hug, and said, 'Why Galldora, wherever have you been! I've been looking for you everywhere and I thought you were really lost for good this time.' Marybell had quite forgotten that she had left Galldora in the tall tree.

Galldora and the Important Document

One day Marybell was giving Galldora, her rag doll, a lesson. They were seated together on the window seat in the nursery, but Galldora kept on flopping forward or backward. At last Marybell said, 'Oh, Galldora, you are a very, very naughty doll. I don't believe you pay any attention to the lessons I give you. Here I have been trying to make you spell and all the time your head keeps lolling back and your eyes stare up at the ceiling. Now, I'll get you all settled again, and if your head goes back once more I'll – I'll – well, I'll have to think of finding some other way of educating you. Because, you know, you are getting old and ugly, you poor old thing, so you've got to be clever.'

Galldora was sat up again, and the large book was put in front of her.

'Now, look, Galldora,' said Marybell, 'look,

you see it's a picture of a cat, and it spells C-A-T.'

Yes, I can see it is a cat, said Galldora to herself. It is very like our 'Your Grace', the black cat. But I am not fond of 'Your Grace' at the moment; he will keep sitting on me when he wants to go to sleep. And now I come to think of it, I don't really like cats all that much, except Bobo, the stuffed cat, so why should I learn how to spell *them*. They can learn how to spell *me*.

Marybell turned over the page. 'Look, Galldora, a cow, and it spells C-O-W.'

Well, I know I don't like cows, went on Galldora to herself. They are too big and too clumsy, and I've been trodden on by cows lots of times when I have been lost, and so I certainly won't learn how to spell cows.

While Galldora was thinking all this to herself, Marybell was saying 'C-O-W' over and over again. Galldora, having made up her mind that she was not going to learn how to spell cow, lost interest in the book, and *plonk*, her head rolled back once more and there she was, with her shoe-button eye staring up at the ceiling.

Marybell suddenly noticed this. She picked Galldora up and said, 'Well, that's that. I won't even try to make you educated, Galldora. I'm very, very cross.'

She took Galldora out of the nursery and walked down the stairs with her. But, on arriving in the hall, Marybell wasn't sure what to do with Galldora. Then she saw her father's brief-case leaning up against the umbrella stand.

That's it, she thought, I'll send my Galldora to daddy's office. She is bound to learn very interesting things there, because my daddy is very, very clever. Mummy thinks so too, I know, for I've heard her saying, 'You are clever, darling.'

Quickly Marybell packed Galldora into the brief-case. First of all she squeezed Galldora as thin as she could by jumping up and down on her. Then she laid Galldora flat in the back of the brief-case, as flat as she could. Even so, Galldora did seem to make the brief-case bulge. So Marybell pulled out Galldora and her daddy's plastic mackintosh that he always kept in his brief-case. Marybell hid the plastic mackintosh behind the umbrella stand, put Galldora back, and examined the brief-case once again. It looked just ordinary.

Marybell whispered into the brief-case, 'There you are, Galldora, you are all right now. And I am sure you will learn to be clever in daddy's office.'

Suddenly Marybell's daddy came into the hall in a great hurry. He was talking all the time to Marybell's mummy as he pulled on his coat.

'Don't worry about me, darling,' he kept saying. Then he turned to Marybell. 'And look after your mummy, won't you, while I'm away.'

'Away?' Marybell gasped. She turned very white and she was just going to say, 'I'd better take Galldora out of the brief-case if you are going away,' but her daddy was talking again to her mummy, while he snatched up the brief-case. He gave a kiss, first to Marybell's mummy and then to Marybell. Then he was out of the house before Marybell could explain about Galldora.

When Marybell's daddy had gone, Marybell stood very silent and very still.

'Cheer up, Marybell,' said Marybell's mummy kindly. 'Daddy will soon be home. Come and help me wash up in the kitchen and I'll help you make some toffee later when I have the time.'

'Oh, Mummy,' said Marybell, 'I'm just dreadfully worried. Oh, poor Galldora!'

'Galldora!' exclaimed Marybell's mummy. 'What's Galldora got to do with it?'

'Well, you see, Mummy, I put Galldora in Daddy's brief-case to make her clever; I mean, because she won't learn any lessons with me. So I thought she might learn to be clever in Daddy's office. I didn't know he was going away.'

Marybell's mother smiled, 'Oh, well, never mind, Marybell,' she said. 'Galldora will have a nice time, because Daddy's going in an aeroplane.'

'An aeroplane. Oh, poor Galldora, it's getting worse and worse.'

'Yes, an aeroplane. I think Galldora would love that, don't you?'

'I don't know, Mummy. Oh, I do hope Daddy looks after my poor Galldora. I just couldn't bear it if something happened to her and I never saw her again, and oh, Mummy, she may get air-sick.'

'I'm sure Daddy will look after Galldora, he's very fond of her, you know that. He's often said he likes her better than any of your other dolls. Oh, and I am quite certain Galldora won't get air-sick, Marybell. I'm quite certain.'

'Yes, Mummy. You may be right.'

Marybell thought she had better not say anything about the mackintosh just then. She'd tell her mother later. Anyway what did a mackintosh matter when poor, dear Galldora was being rushed farther and farther away by train and aeroplane to somewhere far away, where there would be no dolls or teddies to talk to – only businessmen.

Actually Galldora was not at all alarmed or at all worried. At first she heard the chit-chat of the train as it bounced over the rails. It seemed to her to be saying, 'Oh, look, a rag doll, a rag doll, a rag doll, a rag-rag-rag-raggity-rag doll.'

It's very nice of this train to be taking an interest in me like this, thought Galldora, but it does get a bit tiring when that's all he says. Though perhaps, poor train, he's very stupid like me, and that is all he can say.

Galldora, still tucked down comfortably in the leather brief-case, soon realized they were out of the train, and she was being carried along.

Then Galldora knew she was in a bus, for she heard someone saying, 'Yes, that's right, sir, this is the bus for the airport.' All around her she kept hearing people saying, 'bus', 'airport', 'aeroplane', and 'flying'.

Oh, said Galldora to herself. Oh, I wonder if I too am going to an airport and then into an aeroplane. I've often seen pictures of airports and aeroplanes in Marybell's picture books, but I've never seen a real one or been in an aeroplane. I wonder what it feels like.

Galldora was soon to know. At the airport she heard the great pantings and roar of the aeroplanes, though, of course, she could see nothing.

Seems to me, thought Galldora, this is a place where they keep dragons not aeroplanes. What a noise there is. I wonder if fire is coming out of the dragons' noses, as it does in Marybell's picture books.

Then suddenly Galldora felt a very queer feeling. Oh, dear! Oh, dear! I'm going up and up just as if I was with Marybell in the swing.

But after a while the 'going-up' feeling stopped. This is rather fun, thought Galldora, I must be in an aeroplane. Of course, that's what it is, I am in a real aeroplane. They weren't dragons, they were aeroplanes, and I'm right up in the air now, higher than the clouds. How exciting, only I do wish I could see. It is a bit stuffy in this old brief-case; it's making me quite sleepy . . .

Galldora must have dozed off, for the next thing she remembered she was being taken out of the brief-case by a strange man. He stared at Galldora and then said, 'Here, Ted, come and have a look at this.'

Another strange man came and stared at Galldora.

'Well,' exclaimed the second man, called Ted, 'better put it back, Sid.'

'Not on your life,' answered Sid. 'Just think of it, a grown man carrying around a rag doll! Ought to be ashamed of himself. I'll just put her on the table at his place, that'll teach him.'

'It's a bit unkind,' said Ted. 'Maybe it is his mascot. Some chaps have funny mascots. A friend of mine carried round a ball of knitting wool, green it was. Said it always brought him luck. Go on, put it back. Anyway, you shouldn't have looked in his case. Go on, now, put her back.'

But Galldora was not put back, she was propped up on the table. Galldora found it was a very large table, with a great many chairs drawn up to the table, and in front of each chair were papers.

Soon the door opened and a lot of men came in. They all started to sit down around the table. Marybell's daddy gasped when he saw Galldora sitting staring at him. He hurriedly hid her under the table as best he could.

Galldora lay under the table listening to everything that was said. This is going to educate me, she told herself, and then I'll be clever.

She listened and listened and listened but she couldn't really understand a word.

Are they all talking extra Double Dutch, Galldora wondered. I know they are not talking French, because Alouette, the French doll, talks French, and this doesn't sound a bit like her way of talking. I can understand the words all right, but the words don't seem to make sense.

At last Galldora gave up trying to understand.

Well, anyway, this is a very nice way of learning, she consoled herself, because, as I don't understand a word they are talking about, I don't really need to listen. I'm very happy not paying attention.

So Galldora lay under the table while the businessmen and Marybell's daddy discussed business. She was left there, too, when the businessmen got up from the table and went away. She was quite forgotten. Even Marybell's daddy had forgotten all about her.

Galldora was not the only thing left lying under the table, a document was lying there as well. Whether it had been slipped under the table on purpose or by accident, was never certain, but what was certain was that it was a very, very important document.

After many hours a nice plump woman came into the room to tidy up. She found Galldora and the document.

'Well, hello,' she said to Galldora, 'and who might you be?' Galldora liked her at once. She seemed to understand all about dolls, and how they liked to be sat up comfortably and not thrown in corners or on floors.

'There you are, luv,' she said to Galldora, 'you rest there till the morrow and I'll see about you then, when I give the room a turn out. It's just a frisk about I do in the evenings. Don't you fret, luv, I'll find out who you belong to.'

Galldora was placed on a small side-table, firmly seated on the document, and propped up by a huge vase of flowers. She looked quite part of the decorations, and even more so as one of the chrysanthemums dropped and half-hid her.

Suddenly, when the building was quiet and only the stars peeped in through the long win-

dows, two men came creeping into the room. They didn't turn up the lights. They flashed torches about, mostly under the table. They were whispering to each other. Galldora thought they reminded her more of rats than anything else.

I think they are thieves or spies, thought Galldora. I wonder if they are doll thieves? Then, after a think, she felt better. I've never heard of doll thieves, and I'm sure if there were doll thieves my own dear Marybell would have warned me.

The men didn't seem to be able to find what they were looking for. They walked round the large table, flashing their torch-lights.

'It's got to be somewhere,' one of them said.

The other one muttered in a very snarly way, 'It had better be. We've got to find it quick, see?'

A torch-light moving round the walls rested for a second on Galldora. 'Hi! A doll, what do you know!'

'Get on with it,' snarled the man, still searching round the big table. 'Stop fooling around. It's a document we're looking for, not dolls.'

Galldora, who was very frightened, was thankful when the torch-light moved on.

There were footsteps outside and loud talking. The door opened. The two men turned like rats and hid behind the slowly opening door. Then they were out of the room, through the open door, and clattering down the stairs, before the two newcomers could catch them.

One of the newcomers switched on all the lights. Galldora, with a sigh of relief, realized it was Marybell's daddy.

'Funny,' said Marybell's daddy, 'I wonder what they were up to? Odd, the way they were in the dark. I didn't see who they were, did you, John?'

'I did catch a glimpse of them when you turned the lights on, but I can't say I have seen either of them before. No, I'm sure I haven't. Nasty looking fellows.'

'Well, I don't know,' said Marybell's daddy, bewildered. 'They behaved as if they were thieves, yet there isn't a safe in this room, is there?'

'No. Better get that doll of your daughter's, and then we'll report the men,' said the man called John.

'Yes,' said Marybell's daddy. 'Funny though. . . .' He looked under the table but, of course, Galldora wasn't there. 'The room has been tidied up,' he said. 'Still, the doll must have been put somewhere. My little daughter will never forgive me if I lose her rag doll.' Marybell's daddy started looking round the room.

'Ah, there she is,' cried Marybell's daddy, finding Galldora. As he picked Galldora up he noticed the document she had been sitting on.

'Hello, hello,' he murmured softly, then he whistled. 'Here, come and look at this, John.'

The two men stared at the document together.

'How on earth did this get lost?' gasped the man called John. 'My father would blow up if he knew this wasn't in the safe. Why, it is the most important document we've ever had.'

Marybell's father was frowning. 'Why, of course, John, this is what those men were searching for. My word, if this got into the wrong hands. . . . Do you think they were paid to get it?'

Marybell's father stopped, appalled at the idea.

'Well, they never got it,' said the man called John, then he gave a short loud laugh. 'Why, that rag doll of your daughter's saved this precious document. don't you see, she was sitting on it, and clearly the men didn't see it under her.'

'Well done, Galldora,' said Marybell's father softly. 'Well done!' Galldora felt very proud.

'Tell you what,' said the man called John, 'let's make her the firm's mascot.'

'Oh, no! I am afraid you can't do that,' answered Marybell's father. 'My daughter would be broken-hearted if she didn't get her rag doll back.'

'Well, I insist anyway that we make her our mascot for tonight. We'll round up the boys and we'll all go out and celebrate, have the best dinner possible in the best hotel, and we'll take the rag doll with us.'

'Right,' Marybell's father answered. Then he suddenly became very like a little boy. He picked Galldora up and danced with her all round the room.

The two men returned the document to the right person, who put it in the right safe, and the three of them went out to celebrate.

The dinner was wonderful, and a band played all the time. Galldora sat in the middle of the table, and though she felt very sleepy before the end, she kept thinking, I like being a

mascot. I like it very much, and how right
Marybell was to know this was the best way to
educate me.

On the way home the man named John insisted that Galldora was propped up so she
could see out of the window in the aeroplane.

Oh, what a lovely trip, thought Galldora, and
though I'm not beautiful, all the dolls and

teddies in the nursery will listen to every word I say, for none of them have ever been a mascot, or sat on an important document, or seen out of a real aeroplane. I'm very, very lucky – and I do like businessmen, even though they do talk Double Dutch, and are not nearly so clever as my own Marybell.

Galldora and the Train Ride

One day Marybell took Galldora on a train ride. Marybell was going to have tea with her friend Jane. Jane lived in the small town of Tanminster, which was four miles away from Marybell's home. Marybell's mother rang up Jane's mother, and they decided that Marybell could be put on the train at Merryfields station by her mother, and Jane and Jane's mother would be waiting for her at Tanminster station.

Marybell was very excited.

'I'll take Galldora for company,' she told her mother, 'not one of my new dolls, because Galldora is so old it won't matter if the train soot gets all over her, and I think it will be very good for her education, don't you, Mummy?'

'Of course it will, dear,' said Marybell's mother, 'and remember Marybell, it's the next station.'

So Marybell and Galldora were put on the train. It was a small train on a branch line.

When the train pulled up at Tanminster, Marybell got very muddled. 'This doesn't look at all like the town where Jane lives,' she told Galldora, 'and I can't see Jane or her mummy anywhere.'

In fact, there was no one on the station platform but the guard. Marybell tried to read the name of the station but she couldn't quite spell it out. She then thought of asking the guard. But it was too late. With a whistle from the guard and an answering whistle from the engine the train slowly rumbled on.

'It must have been a station Mummy forgot about,' said Marybell.

Marybell did not know that Jane and Jane's mother arrived just as the train was moving out of the station. They thought Marybell had missed the train.

'Or perhaps she had a lift by car after all,' said Jane.

'We'll go home and ring up,' said Jane's mother.

When Jane's mother did ring up Marybell's mother was out.

In the train was Marybell with Galldora propped up against the window to see the view. It was a wonderful sunny day, so sunny it was quite stuffy in the train.

I shall be very glad when we get out, thought Galldora. I am sure the sun will melt my shoe-button eyes.

The train went, 'Sing-me-a-song – bump-me-along – sing-me-a-song,' and the noise was so like a lullaby and the carriage was so warm and stuffy Marybell fell into a doze.

At last with a violent jerk they drew up at the next station.

Marybell woke up and jumped out of the train with Galldora. She stood on the platform for a moment, but there was neither Jane nor her mother. The guard had gone to join a friend in a small black shed for a cup of tea, as it was the last station on the small branch line. The engine was shunting down a side rail and getting ready to pull the train all the way back again. The man who took the tickets, thinking there were no tickcts to take, had wandered up the platform, watering the flower-beds with a huge watering-can.

So Marybell and Galldora just walked out of the station. They wandered down a road, a strange road that neither of them had ever seen before. There were high trees on either side, and turtle doves were purring.

'I don't know where we are,' said Marybell, 'and I am getting very hungry.'

Oh dear! thought Galldora, how unfortunate.

There didn't seem to be any houses in sight, and the road went up and up a long hill and it grew darker and greener all the time.

Marybell got a stone in her sandal, so she had to sit at the side of the road, take off her sandal, and shake out the stone. When Marybell put her shoe on again and got up she quite forgot to pick up Galldora. Galldora lay at the side of the road and watched Marybell go on and on and on, and disappear round a bend. Galldora's shoe-button eyes grew misty.

Life, said Galldora to herself, can be very sad. And she lay there, alone and forgotten, for a long time.

After an hour – it must have been quite an hour – a gipsy cart came by. A piebald pony was harnessed to an open cart, and in the cart were four children. The children's mother was driving the cart. They were coming down the hill.

'Mum! Mum!' shouted one of the children. 'What's that, there, on the side – see?'

Now, gipsies are like squirrels, they can't bear to see anything just lying about. They have to go and pick it up and keep it. After all, everything comes in useful at one time or another. So the cart stopped, and Galldora was picked up.

'I want it!' shouted one of the children.

'It's mine – I saw it first, didn't I?' said the boy who had seen Galldora.

'Go on, give it to her,' said an elder boy. 'What do you want with a doll, anyway?' So Galldora was taken up and examined very thoroughly by the youngest gipsy child. Galldora's eyes were pulled and nearly came off. Galldora's hair was pulled, and some of it did come off.

'Dear me,' sighed poor Galldora, 'this is not at all nice. Still, I'm seeing life, and it's all good for my education.'

The gipsies soon passed the station. But they didn't stop. On went the gipsy cart for quite a while and then it turned off the road.

Galldora found herself being taken out of the cart by her new owner. Soon she was seated down by a gipsy fire. Round the fire were three men – one older man and two young men. The young men were very gay. Their clothes were newish, and the handkerchiefs round their necks were brightly coloured; and their hats were set at a jaunty angle. The older man had a faded but still dashing look about him. A greyhound was sitting by his feet.

As soon as the greyhound saw Galldora he started to ripple all his muscles, and pointed out his long, thin snout to sniff. Then the greyhound slowly started to rise, but the man shouted, 'Get down, there,' and the animal sank down again.

'Well, thank goodness for that,' said Galldora.

The woman, whose gold ear-rings flashed in the firelight, put a great saucepan on the flames. Her hair and her apron were as black as Galldora's eyes. Looking at her, Galldora thought how handsome she looked.

'I'm very glad now that my eyes are black,' said Galldora, 'because I can see that black is a very becoming colour.'

Galldora was not left long to sit and gaze ahead. A little bantam cock came strutting up.

He stood on one foot and stared at Galldora with one eye. The three wives of the bantam cock, all chatting at once, kept saying, 'What is it? Is it good to eat? Let's have a go.'

'Keep back,' ordered the bantam cock, 'and let me try first.' He came and took a peck at Galldora and said, 'Quite disgusting,' and with that he turned his beautiful plumed tail on Galldora and strutted away. The wives, after casting a disapproving look at Galldora, hurried after the cock.

Then, when no one was looking, Galldora was pounced on by a puppy. The puppy was clearly a puppy of no pedigree and no finer feelings, for he tossed and worried poor Galldora quite terribly. His teeth were sharp, and his claws were sharp too. Galldora thought lovingly of Marybell's spaniel, Sparks, for Sparks had a soft mouth and, though he loved to play with Galldora, he did it more in a pretending way than a real way.

Still, thought Galldora, we can't always expect an easy life, and she put up with the puppy's excited bitings and scratchings in a very gallant way. At last the puppy was thrown a bone, which he found more to his liking than Galldora, and he ran away, leaving Galldora very near the great fire.

Poor Galldora was nearly burned. Her dress and one side of her head was quite singed. As she lay there, Galldora thought of Marybell. I do hope she has found something to eat, Galldora kept on thinking.

Marybell had. Marybell was very happy. She was sitting up at a large table. Spread before her was cream and a honeycomb and lots of butter and scones, and a soft boiled egg, and ham.

'This is just the kind of meal I like best,' Marybell was saying between each mouthful.

Sitting opposite Marybell was a small, wrinkled old lady. She looked exactly like a stored-away Cox's apple that was forgotten in an attic. The old lady kept on looking at Marybell and saying, 'Well, I don't know what to do for the best, I'm sure.'

On the floor by the kitchen range was a little tabby cat and, playing by her, were two kittens

with very tabby markings and very blue eyes. In the window was a round-looking wire cage, and in the cage sat a very moth-eaten-looking parrot. And every time the little old lady said 'I don't know what to do for the best, I'm sure,' the parrot whistled *Pop goes the Weasel*. He whistled it very well, but he just couldn't get the end bit right, which seemed to worry him. He would pause a moment and then say, 'Me-ow,' just like the cats.

'If it wasn't for me rheumatics,' at last said

the little old lady, 'I'd know what to do, but there – I'm a martyr to 'em.'

'I like it here,' said Marybell, who always liked other people's houses. Marybell looked at the window-sill and said, 'I think you are very clever to grow a beautiful red flower like that.'

'Ah, that's me cactus love, and it likes the warm as I do.'

'Up and down the City Road,' sang the parrot.

Marybell helped herself to a huge slice of cherry-cake.

As Marybell was munching her fourth bit of cake, and the little old lady was saying, still staring at Marybell, 'I wish I knew what to do for the best, I do, really.' Marybell's daddy, a very worried, grey-looking daddy, was standing by the gipsy fire.

'No, sir,' the older of the gipsy men was saying, 'we've seen no girl hereabouts. Not today, have we, Vi?' The gipsy woman called Vi shook her head till her ear-rings rattled.

Marybell's daddy let his eyes wander to the cart. The gipsies had made a kind of hidden room under the cart by draping a waterproof cloth over the edges. The gipsy woman, noticing Marybell's daddy gazing at the improvised room, laughed.

'You don't think I'd keep her if I found her, do you sir?' she said. 'I've got enough of my own.'

'Oh, well,' said Marybell's daddy, 'I'd better drive back to the station.'

'She couldn't have gone farther than here, the train goes no farther,' said one of the young men.

'I know,' said Marybell's daddy. He was very dispirited. Just then the puppy caught sight of Galldora's eyes sparkling in the firelight. He pounced and dragged Galldora out.

'What have you got?' called one of the young men. All eyes were turned on the puppy and Galldora.

'Why!' cried Marybell's daddy excitedly, 'that's her doll!'

The young man took Galldora away from the puppy and handed it to Marybell's daddy.

'Yes,' said Marybell's daddy, 'this is her doll, Galldora. I'd know her anywhere.'

'We found it up on the hill, past the station,' said the gipsy woman.

'You couldn't show me where that was exactly?' asked Marybell's daddy.

'One of the kids will go along with you, sir,' said the gipsy woman, 'he'd be pleased to have a ride in a car, and he can walk home.'

But all four gipsy children wanted to go, so the four children and the puppy and Galldora went in the car.

The car stopped where Galldora had been found, and the gipsy children and the puppy got out. Marybell's daddy gave them a shilling each, which pleased them, and they waved him on his way with large friendly grins.

The car went on up the hill and round the bend till it came to a small cottage. It was a tiny, two-roomed cottage standing all alone, in a kind of lost way, at the side of the road. In the window was a parrot in a cage and a giant cactus, with a huge red cactus-flower. Marybell's daddy knocked at the door.

'Come in,' called a high, thin voice, and Marybell's daddy went in. At first he could hardly see, for the heat of the room seemed to sting his eyes, and then he could hardly see because he was being hugged so much.

'I'm so glad you've come,' said Marybell, 'because I was just beginning to be lost, and Mrs Robins and I were wondering what to do for the best.'

Marybell's daddy was so happy at finding Marybell that he quite forgot to scold her. He thanked little old Mrs Robins, who said, 'Marybell must come for tea again one day.'

Then Marybell climbed into her daddy's car and was driven home. Marybell was very tired, and fell asleep in the car, but before she fell asleep she said, 'I'm glad I'm found and I promise I'll never go for a train ride on my own again.'

'You'd better thank Galldora,' said Marybell's daddy, 'for if it hadn't been for her I might not have found you for a very long time.'

'Galldora's a very clever doll,' said Marybell, hugging Galldora. 'She's my very favourite doll, although she's so old.'

It's all this travelling that has made me clever,

thought Galldora to herself. My education is coming on very well, I think, but all the same, I'm very glad Marybell is not going to take me for a train ride all by herself again. It gave me quite a fright.

By the same author

THE ADVENTURES OF GALLDORA

Although Marybell loved Galldora very much, she wasn't always very careful to look after her, so that Galldora was always getting lost. She was lost in a field with a scarecrow, lost on top of a roof, and lost in all sorts of other strange places.

It was very inconvenient to be lost so often, but it did teach her a good deal about the world, and as Galldora sensibly said, 'A doll's got to have something, and if she hasn't got looks, education is useful'.

Some Other Young Puffins for 5 and 6 year olds

CLEVER POLLY AND THE STUPID WOLF
POLLY AND THE WOLF AGAIN
Catherine Storr

Clever Polly manages to think of lots of good ideas to stop the stupid wolf from eating her.

GOBBOLINO, THE WITCH'S CAT
Ursula Moray Williams

Gobbolino's mother was ashamed of him because his eyes were blue instead of green, and he wanted to be loved instead of learning spells. So he went in search of a friendly kitten.

THE HAPPY ORPHELINE
Natalie Savage Carlson

The twenty little orphaned girls who live with Madame Flattot are terrified of being adopted because they are so happy.

A BROTHER FOR THE ORPHELINES
Natalie Savage Carlson

Sequel to *The Happy Orpheline*. Josine, the smallest of all the orphans, finds a baby left on the doorstep. But he is a *boy*. So the orphans plot and worry to find a way to keep him.

A GIFT FROM WINKLESEA
Helen Cresswell

Dan and Mary buy a beautiful stone like an egg as a present for their mother – and then it hatches out, into the oddest animal they ever saw.

THE TEN TALES OF SHELLOVER
MORE TALES OF SHELLOVER
Ruth Ainsworth

Shellover the tortoise tells one story for each of the creatures in Mrs Candy's garden.

ROBIN
Catherine Storr

Robin was the youngest of three, and hated it. And then he discovered the shell called the Freedom of the Seas – and became the wonder of his family.

MISS HAPPINESS AND MISS FLOWER
Rumer Godden

Nona was lonely far away from her home in India, and the two dainty Japanese dolls, Miss Happiness and Miss Flower, were lonely too. But once Nona started building them a proper Japanese house they all felt better.

MAGIC IN MY POCKET
Alison Uttley

A selection of short stories by this well-loved author, especially good for five and six year olds.

THE DOLLS' HOUSE
Rumer Godden

Mr and Mrs Plantaganet and their family were very happy in their antique dolls' house, until Marchpane the elegant, selfish china doll moved in with them and acted as if she owned the place.

THE SECRET SHOEMAKERS

James Reeves

A dozen of Grimms' least-known fairy tales retold with all a poet's magic, and illustrated sympathetically by Edward Ardizzone.

TALES FROM THE END COTTAGE
MORE TALES FROM THE END COTTAGE

Eileen Bell

Two tabby cats and a Peke live with Mrs Apple in a Northampton-shire cottage. They quarrel, have adventures and entertain dangerous strangers. A new author with a special·talent for writing about animals. For reading aloud to 5 and over, private reading 7 plus. (*Original*).

GEORGE

Agnes Sligh Turnbull

George was good at arithmetic, and housekeeping, and at keeping children happy and well behaved. The pity of it was that he was a rabbit so Mr Weaver didn't believe in him. Splendid for six year olds and over.

THE YOUNG PUFFIN BOOK OF VERSE

Barbara Ireson

A deluge of poems about such fascinating subjects as birds and bal-loons, mice and moonshine, farmers and frogs, pigeons and pirates, especially chosen to please young children of four to eight. (*Original*)

DEAR TEDDY ROBINSON
ABOUT TEDDY ROBINSON
KEEPING UP WITH TEDDY ROBINSON
TEDDY ROBINSON HIMSELF

Joan G. Robinson

Teddy Robinson was Deborah's teddy bear and such a very nice, friendly, cuddly bear that he went everywhere with her – and had even more adventures than she did.

LITTLE OLD MRS PEPPERPOT
MRS PEPPERPOT TO THE RESCUE
MRS PEPPERPOT IN THE MAGIC WOOD
MRS PEPPERPOT'S OUTING

Alf Prøysen

Gay little stories about an old woman who suddenly shrinks to the size of a pepperpot.

DANNY FOX

David Thomson

How clever Danny Fox helps the princess marry the fisherman she loves, and gets food for his children, Lick, Chew and Swallow. (*Original*)

DANNY FOX MEETS A STRANGER

David Thomson

More Danny Fox adventures. This time he has to cope with the Stranger, a sinister greedy wolf who wants to steal his home and hunting ground (*Original*)

THE PENNY PONY

Barbara Willard

Life is never quite the same for Cathy and Roger after they find the penny pony in Mrs Boddy's shop.

ALBERT

Alison Jezard

Adventures of a nice cheerful bachelor bear who lives in the East End of London.

THE URCHIN

Edith Unnerstad

The Urchin is only five years old – but already he has the Larsson family at sixes and sevens with his ingenious tricks and adventures.

LITTLE O

Edith Unnerstad

The enchanting story of the youngest of the Pip Larsson family.

FIVE DOLLS IN A HOUSE

Helen Clare

A little girl called Elizabeth finds a way of making herself small and visits her dolls in their own house.

SOMETHING TO DO

Septima

This is a book full of suggestions for games to play and things to make and do each month, from January to December. It is designed to help mothers with young children at home. (*Original*)

SOMETHING TO MAKE

Felicia Law

A varied and practical collection of things for children to make from the odds and ends around the house, with very little extra outlay, by an experienced teacher of art and handicrafts. For children of 6 up. (*Original*)